Seriously Silly Stories

SHAMPOOZEL

Compass Point Books
3109 West 50th Street, #115
Minneapolis, MN 55410

Visit Compass Point Books on the Internet at *www.compasspointbooks.com*
or e-mail your request to *custserv@compasspointbooks.com*

Library of Congress Cataloging-in-Publication Data
Anholt, Laurence.
  Shampoozel / by Laurence Anholt. Illustrated by Arthur Robins.
    p. cm. — (Seriously silly stories)
Summary: In this version of the classic fairy tale "Rapunzel," the daughter of two hair-
dressers is locked in a tower by the Bad Hair Witch.
ISBN 0-7565-0634-4 (hardcover)
  [1. Fairy tales. 2. Humorous stories.] I. Title II. Series: Anholt, Laurence. Seriously
silly stories.
  PZ8.A577Sh 2004
  [E]—dc22   2003017956

For more information on *Shampoozel,* use FactHound
to track down Web sites related to this book.

  1. Go to *www.compasspointbooks.com/facthound*
  2. Type in this book ID: 0756506344
  3. Click on the *Fetch It* button.

Your trusty FactHound will fetch the best Web sites for you!

About the Author
Laurence Anholt is one of the UK's leading authors. From his home in
Dorset, he has produced more than 80 books, which are published all
around the world. His Seriously Silly Stories have won numerous
awards, including the Smarties Gold Award for "Snow White and the
Seven Aliens."

About the Illustrator
Arthur Robins has illustrated more than 50 picture books, all of them
highly successful and popular titles, and is the illustrator for all the
Seriously Silly Stories. His energetic and fun-filled drawings have been
featured in countless magazines, advertisements, and animations. He
lives with his wife and two daughters in Surrey, England.

First published in Great Britain by Orchard Books, 96 Leonard Street, London EC2A 4XD

Text © Laurence Anholt 1999/Illustrations © Arthur Robins 1999

Printed in the United States of America.
03038 6849

Seriously Silly Stories

SHAMPOOZEL

Written by Laurence Anholt
Illustrated by Arthur Robins

COMPASS POINT BOOKS
Minneapolis, Minnesota

4

There was once a happy hairdresser named Dan Druff.

Dan LOVED hair!

Curly hair and bristly hair, eyebrows and beards—Dan loved them all. He loved the gleam of his many mirrors and the snippety-snick of sparkling silver scissors.

Dan even sang about hair.

Hair, hair, glorious hair,
It spreads from your head,
Nearly EVERYWHERE.

It grows on your toes,
Even inside your nose,
Hair, hair, HA-A-A-I-I-R!!

Only one thing upset Dan's happiness—his girlfriend, Tam O'Tei, who lived in the apartment upstairs.

Unlike Dan, Tam was a sad person who hid away in her bedroom behind tightly closed curtains. From under their hair dryers, Dan's customers could hear her wretched moans and Dan nearly tore his hair out with worry over her condition.

The awful truth was...

…Tam O'Tei had terrible hair!

"Oh, Dan," she wailed. "My hair is dull and lifeless. I have a flaky scalp and unsightly split ends, but no ordinary shampoo is effective."

Dan could find nothing to help, and as the days passed, Tam's hair grew as greasy as a fast food mop.

Now, not far from the barbershop was an evil black tower, which twisted into the sky like a strange hairstyle.

This was the home of the Bad Hair Witch.

High in her dark rooms, the Bad Hair Witch mixed strange shampoos and conditioners, which were sold all over the world. The secret ingredients came from rare plants that grew only in her private garden.

Above the barbershop, Tam became convinced that one of these magical hair herbs would bring life back to her dull scalp, and she pleaded with Dan to pick some.

At the mention of the black tower, Dan Druff felt the hairs prickle at the back of his neck.

"I can't go there," he whispered. "What if I fall into the evil hair-grip of the Bad Hair Witch?"

But Tam O'Tei complained so long and hard that at last Dan Druff couldn't stand it any longer. "All right, keep your hair on," he bristled. "I will go to the tower and comb the gardens for your herbs."

So the next morning, before dawn, the brave barber crept reluctantly up the hairpin bends that led to the tower.

As he walked, he sang to keep up his courage.

17

Before he could finish his song, Dan had almost walked into a huge sign hanging on the wall before him:

Dan felt a shiver run along his moustache. Only the thought of Tam's sad locks drove him on. Ignoring the sign, he scrambled into the Bad Hair Witch's secret garden where he found a second sign:

DAN DRUFF, CAN'T YOU READ? DON'T EVEN THINK ABOUT STEALING A WEED

Poor Dan had never been in such a hairy situation, but he bent down and began to stuff his pockets with the herbs.

Suddenly he heard a terrible voice:

"Dan Druff, you must be crazy,
You'll pay for those plants,
With your very first baby."

Dan's hair stood on end—it was the worst rhyme he had ever heard.

Before him stood… the Bad Hair Witch!

"B-but I don't have a b-baby," stammered Dan.

"Well, let's not split hairs," snapped the witch. "I will wait until your first child is born."

Grabbing a last handful of herbs, Dan jumped over the wall and hurried down the hill to the town.

He found Tam in her bedroom wearing a paper bag on her head, and he poured out the story of his terrifying brush with the Bad Hair Witch.

But Tam was barely listening. She seized the wonderful herbs, crushed them, and began to lather her scalp…

As if by magic, Tam's hair turned into a glorious mass of glossy curls that seemed to flow in slow motion when she tossed her head.

Tam O'Tei was cured!

She tore downstairs into the sunny shop, and, as Dan shaved the bristly early morning customers, Tam happily set to work beside him, sweeping up the fallen curls and locks.

That very week, Tam and Dan were married, and the whole town joined them in this glorious hymn:

Hair, hair, MAGNIFICENT hair,
It can grow down below,
    past your underwear.
It grows on your chest,
Like a big woolly nest.
Hair, hair, HA-A-A-I-I-R!!

29

Before a year was out, the couple's happiness was complete—a beautiful baby daughter was born, and, after much thought, they called her...

In that happy hairy world, not one thought was given to the Bad Hair Witch.

But the Bad Hair Witch had forgotten nothing.

High in her tower she worked day and night on her most amazing invention yet—something all barbers dream of—a marvelous, magical HAIR GROWING LOTION!

32

"Guess which witch will be rich?" she sniggered. "All I need is a helpless, hairless baby to test my invention."

And so the Bad Hair Day dawned. The bell at the little barbershop tinkled cruelly as the Bad Hair Witch burst inside.

"Give me the child!" she shrieked.

"Have you got an appointment?" said Tam. "Let's see, I could fit you in on Thursday…"

"You don't understand, you fools. I need to test my new improved formula— Ultimate 2-in-1 Hair Growing Lotion."

"Leave Shampoozel alone," pleaded Tam O'Tei. "You cannot try out your hair-brained inventions on our child."

Ignoring the tears of the unfortunate couple, the Bad Hair Witch seized Shampoozel and carried her back to the tower.

To make sure the precious child would never be taken from her, the Hair Witch bricked up the front door behind them.

As the days passed, the Bad Hair Witch grew to love the baby and looked after her as if she were her own.

She would sing as she washed the infant's hair:

No more tears, Baby Shampoozel,
My magic shampoo is very unusual.

And day by day, as Shampoozel grew, her hair grew too, in great long golden tresses that tumbled across the floor, down the stairs, into the kitchen, under the dog, round the back of the fridge and back upstairs again.

"Hair, hair, HAIR!!" cackled the Bad Hair Witch. "Look at all your beautiful golden hair!"

Sometimes hairy Shampoozel remembered her parents' little barbershop in the town far below.

Now that their daughter had gone, Dan and Tam worked sadly and never sang anymore; and so, one by one, the customers went elsewhere.

Years passed, and as Shampoozel grew into a young woman, the Bad Hair Witch taught her the secret art of the hairdresser:

> Wash your hair and keep it sweet.
> Lather, rinse, repeat.
> Rub and comb and keep it neat.
> Lather, rinse, repeat.

Together, the Bad Hair Witch and Shampoozel created new hair products that were more amazing than anyone could have dreamed of.

They became so famous, in fact, that a young prince by the name of Gary Baldie heard about them from his home in a distant land.

The prince, although handsome and wealthy, was as bald as a beach ball.

Prince Gary had tried one wig-maker after another but without satisfaction, so when he finally heard about Ultimate 2-in-1 Hair Growing Lotion, he set out right away, and after many days arrived at the tower.

Of course, even a prince cannot enter a tower without a door. So Prince Gary concealed himself beneath the walls and after a while he saw an amazing thing.

The Bad Hair Witch
appeared at the window
with her shopping bag.
All of a sudden a great
mass of hair cascaded
to the ground. The witch
slid down it and set off
toward the town.

"I suppose that's
what they call a hair
slide!" whispered
Prince Gary in
amazement.

47

Half an hour later, the old lady returned
with her shopping and called out:

Shampoozel, Shampoozel,
Let down your hair,
So I can climb to the top
Of your long hairy stair.

Shampoozel let down her locks again, and
the old woman scrambled back up the tower.

Gary Baldie was no fool and the next time the old woman went out, the prince stood below the window himself and called:

Shampoozel, Shampoozel,
Your hair is so curly,
Let it hang down now,
Be a good girlie.

To his delight, a great coil of hair tumbled to the ground. He seized it and began to baldly go where no man had gone before.

The prince scrambled into Shampoozel's room, and when his royal eyes fell on the lovely Shampoozel he was captivated by her hairiness.

He leaned toward her and kissed her ruby red lips.

There and then, Shampoozel and the prince fell in love. Gary told her that he adored her limitless locks, and how he would love to have some of his own.

To his amazement, Shampoozel replied that she had grown tired of her hair. "It half hurts when people climb up it," she complained. "And it takes a week to wash."

But then, to the prince's joy, Shampoozel pulled out a tiny bottle of Ultimate 2-in-1 Hair Growing Lotion and began to massage his shiny scalp.

Almost immediately, a single hair popped out of the prince's head.

The first hair was followed by a second, the second by a third, and within 10 minutes the prince had a mass of golden curls snaking down his back, nearly as long as Shampoozel's.

Gary Baldie seized Shampoozel and danced with joy.

"My prince, you must wash and go," whispered Shampoozel.

She brushed a few stray hairs from his collar, and with one final kiss, the prince climbed down Shampoozel's hair and slipped away into the shadows.

It wasn't long before the Bad Hair Witch returned.

Shampoozel, Shampoozel,
Don't make me shout,
Let down your hair, Girl,
Don't hang about.

As soon as she entered the salon, the witch spotted Gary Baldie's little crown, which Shampoozel had left hanging on the coat hook.

The witch was furious and, after a terrible argument, stormed into her bedroom, leaving Shampoozel weeping pitifully.

The prince, meanwhile, had decided that witch or no witch, he had to see Shampoozel again. He stood at the foot of the tower and whispered:

Shampoozel, Shampoozel,
Here is your prince.
Throw down your pigtail,
My hair needs a rinse.

Immediately, a long lock of hair curled out of the window and tumbled to the ground.

But just as the prince was about climb up, he saw a figure sliding down...

It was Shampoozel!

"I don't know why I didn't think of this before," she said. "All that stupid hair. I cut it off and tied it to the bed. Then I slid down to you. At last we have escaped from the Bad Hair Witch."

"That was a close shave!" replied Gary Baldie, softly stroking her silky stubble. "Come on, let's really let our hair down."

So Shampoozel and her hairy prince ran away to his castle, but she didn't forget her parents, Dan Druff and Tam O'Tei.

Although they were rich, Shampoozel and Gary Baldie liked to work in Dan's shop on Saturdays.

Before long, the little barbershop was once again the busiest in the land.

"It's amazing how the customers keep
coming back," laughed Dan.

And it was true—some of the customers
seemed to have as many as five haircuts a day.

Perhaps they just loved having their hair cut by Shampoozel.

Or perhaps the secret shampoo she uses has something to do with it…

Or perhaps they come for the endless happy songs that drift across the hairy town…

High in her tower, even the Bad Hair Witch joins in:

Hair, hair, SENSATIONAL hair,
Shampoozel's the girl,
To share your hair care.
She can give you a shave,
Or a permanent wa-a-ve,
Hair, HAIR...
H-A-A-A-A-I-I-I-R-R-R!!!!